S0-BIW-018

Darrell King
CEO/Author

Elbert Jones Jr.
COO/Administrator

Publishing Imprint=KJ Publications, Inc.

Motto: "The Future of Urban Fiction"

2292 76309

JAN 2 7 2017

The gavel had scarcely touched down before she had to signal for the noise to stop again. The courthouse was in an uproar as she was about to pronounce the verdict the jury reached on the case. It had been months of constant threats and attacks but at last she would be able to breathe. Her children had to go on a trip just so that they could be safe from all the danger the case brought with its publicity. Sitting as the judge in the case against one of the most notorious Mexican gangster has not been easy on her.

Like most people in the courthouse, they had an idea what the verdict would be. At the beginning of the trial, the jury had been concerned about their safety but after making sure that their details were kept secret, they proceeded to do their civic duty. They jury was housed just few streets away from the courthouse so that there would be no need for long transportation. Three cars were always available to pick them up from their hotel rooms and return them at the end of each court session. They never had to ride in the car because; they took shortcuts between houses to get to court. That way everyone's attention would always be fixed on the car that was filled with security personnel dressed as civilians.

They had been meeting for six days after the attorneys had both given their closing arguments. T.V. crews stationed their vans at the entrance to the court with their reporters loitering around the courthouse waiting to get firsthand information on what the verdict could turn out to be. Gang members hung around, coming and going briefly, being careful so that the cops would not notice them. Family members of the murdered victims and friends and families of other victims whose case never made it to court and even those who lost, they were present throughout the case. Always having enough words to say to the press about their expectation that the case would not be dragged for too long and finally dismissed like the other ones, they never forgot to show their sad faces.

He had been in this courtroom more times than he wished. When he was just sixteen and he was caught and charged for assault. Just weeks before his eighteenth birthday, he was caught breaking into someone's home but through all these and worse offences he committed, he conquered them all. This case was one that he had seen and thought he could win and he would have done everything to avoid it only if he knew sooner how hard they were coming for him. Just like everyone he had killed, he always used a knife that he carved himself, giving it every specification that made slicing through throats look easy and fun. He only killed people who offended him, and never those who had no issue with him so in his heart, everyone he'd ever killed was a bad person and he was just there to make sure that there was no increase in the number of bad guys in his area. His crew was a very tight one so no one among them would ever betray him. They have all been rolling together since they were kids and they trusted each other with their lives.

When he was a kid and he lived with his sister, Carlito had always had a vision too become richer than anyone in his family had ever being. His father was a drunk who stayed at home all day and the little money their mother made from the house cleaning job she did was usually spent with their father every evening at the bar. He always had to look for means to feed himself and his sister. He started with helping neighbors clean their gardens, run errands and walk their dogs. When most neighbors saw that they didn't really need his help, he to court. How the cops knew to raid his tattoo parlor was still a mystery to him. He never brought his street business there and for that he never fully trusted any of his former gang members. After five years had passed on the murder, he was now getting arrested for it and as it looks, there was no way he would win this case. His lawyer had told him to plead guilty at the preliminary hearing so that they could go for a plea bargain with the state attorney. He had not listened then because he believed that like every other crime he had been accused of, he would come out victorious.

When he got the notice that he was needed at the courthouse, he knew that the jury had reached a verdict which he was sure would not favor him. He wanted to regret every action he had ever taken starting from when he decided to join the gang but he decided against that. If he landed in prison, he would need to have some rep so that he would survive long enough inside. He could only hope that jury had seen that he was truly sorry for the murders he committed and not sentence him to death. Dressed in the suit his attorney had got for him for the final arguments, he was walked into the courtroom. He looked around him, and although he couldn't recognize most of the people present, he was sure that they were all there to watch his face when the judge announces that his fate had been decided and it was going to be death just like those he took their lives from. He looked at the bereaved faces, the angry faces and the cold stares of people who have lost someone because of him and he realized how unemotional he had been for a long time. Right behind him, his sister was seated. She had been present all through the trial though she had to take care of the tattoo parlor. He knew that she would always be there this time just as she had always been there every time he was in trouble. Her smile put him at ease and with a renewed confidence; he sat down in his seat and waited for the judge to read the verdict.

The judge was banging the gavel once again. The foreman had just handed him the verdict. She just wanted to read the verdict and be done with this case. The attorneys were also tired of waiting to close the case and move on with their lives. The noise died down and everyone was waiting for the judge to read it out.

She looked at it and wondered why? Why would they finally give this kind of judgment? After all the days they took and how long they made everyone wait. She noticed that the crowd was beginning to get restless.

She cleared her throat and the murmur died down. She read out the verdict that was handed to her and there was a shout of victory from everywhere in the corner room but when she completed what was written, most of the noise stopped. The verdict had said that they found Carlito guilty but they were not sentencing him to death, rather they sentenced him to fifty years imprisonment.

He could hardly believe his ears, he was not dying today. He looked back at his sister and saw the tears rolling down her face. He did not have much time to say his goodbyes before he was taken away. He had told her not to come visit him in prison. He needed her to take good care of the business but he knew that she would never let him feel abandoned just because he was in prison.

All this happened two years ago.

In the pool of the new duplex she had recently purchased, Isabella Sanchez also called Diamante and her friends, Natalia, Vanessa and Elisa. In their flowery bikinis, and ice cold dirty banana in hand, they were talking about Natalia's new boyfriend, Henrique. He was a businessman from Chicago who just moved to the area. He was looking to open a new mall in the area but he also wanted to see if he would like the life down in East L.A.

"You should see him with his clothes off; his chest is very broad and oh! He's got a really big pene."

"And in just how many days after you met him did you know that?" Elisa asked amidst the laughter that was roaring.

"I did not do too much bad; it was just that night after I met him. I really tried to resist him but it was just impossible."

"Hey girl, you are such a slut, I am sure you didn't even try to resist. You just love getting banged."

"I can hardly imagine what I would call you then. Slut? You don't expect that after I left that sorry ass of a guy, I would not need someone to keep me in shape? I really needed to know how that felt again."

"I wouldn't dwell too much on anything that has to do with you. You always do right by yourself."

Isabella cut in the argument. If she let them be, they would keep going like that till it was night. "You ladies should know we are all supposed to be good *primo.*" She got out of the pool and wrapped herself in a towel.

"What do you girls say, let's go shopping and let some heat off." She paused and looked at Natalia then continued. "Maybe Naty should call Henrique so that he can sponsor our shopping today; let's see what your *amante* has in store for you." She turned to speak to Vanessa and Elisa like Natalia wasn't there "*Ella esta con su amante porque es rico.*"

They laughed loudly eyeing her as she called Henrique. "Hey *amado*. I just..................."

She stopped mid-sentence looking shocked. She looked up at her friends with tears about to fall from her eyes. She put on a brave face not to give them something to tease her about. "He just would not wait to listen to what I had to say..." she supplied when they seem not to be interested in what just happened. She looked at the pity look they had on their faces but knew that it was fake. The moment she let out her emotions, they would be out with their phones recording everything she did.

"Are we not still going shopping? I can really use it now." they all broke into laughter again then she had no choice, she started crying. After almost laughing their heads off, they came to sit beside her by the pool.

With arms around her, Elisa said, "You are pretty Naty, and why should you be so heartbroken over that *pinche culero*, you have known him only for few days. There are more than enough guys out there who would love to have you."

Tears streaming down her face, she said, "You know I don't like those *guey* frolicking all around me. They piss me off. How often do we get to meet guys like Henrique? I can't just believe that he would care that less about me after what we had."

"Hey Naty, don't keep talking about the great time you guys had together. He's a guy and he has moved on from that night, he doesn't expect that you would still be stuck in it." Isabella said.

"You know what, we are going out, we need to forget what some *hijo de puta* do to us and have fun." They left the pool and went to the living room where they had all left their clothes. Isabella went up to her bedroom to change into something more light.

Soon they were all ready and some minutes past three, they were in Isabella's Porsche on their way to Skeletons in the Closet to do some quick shopping before it was closed. Making a turn into Mission Rd, Naty saw Henrique with another lady. She got enraged and asked Isabella to stop the car. Unknowing to her, she also stopped.

In a mad rage, she ran to meet Henrique and began cursing him. It took her three friends to get her calm but even after that, she wouldn't stop crying. Henrique and the other lady had entered Skeletons in the Closet so they decided to go somewhere else. After driving around a while, they decided to just go to the *Casa de la Tinta* and gist. At least there would be more fun there than having to sit around Naty while she cried all day. The four blonde pretty ladies got out of the Porsche and as they were about to enter the parlor, the door almost hit them in the face.

"Oh my God! Fuck me. I didn't mean to hurt you ladies. I was kinda busy on the phone." He looked round at them before he continued. "Hope I am forgiven?"

They answered at the same time. "Of course......" they could not help but stare. He was such a handsome guy. "Sorry, can I pass?" he asked and it was then they realized they were standing on his way.

They moved away and kept following his every movement till he was out of sight range. They rushed into Isabella's office, all eager to exclaim about what they just saw.

Elisa was the first to speak up. "Who on earth created that guy? He's got a damn well-structured body that I wish to just lay on all day."

Naty was the next to speak. "Forget Henrique. That guy is the bomb! He'd have made my eyes go sore if he hadn't left sooner." "If you girls don't know, it was *flechazo* for me. I have never seen a guy like that." Vanessa added.

They all looked at Isabella and saw that she was not paying attention to them.

"Diamante, did you see that guy?" Vanessa asked.

"What guy?" she asked, still busy with what she was searching for.

"That black handsome guy we met at the door. You know the one with the big chest." She answered.

"Oh! That guy? I have to confess, he was such a sight. But I don't think there's much to think of getting there, he would have a girl already. He's too handsome to be single."

"Who cares if he's seeing someone, as long as he comes to my bed regularly, I am okay with that." Elisa said.

"And I am sure you can imagine that his girlfriend would be a black girl? Are you ready to start a fight with those girls? Let's discuss something else girls."

"What's this *chava* saying? Do you mean you don't find that guy sexy enough to fight over?"

"Seriously babes, let us not dwell on this. I know the guy is super-sexy but I don't think he would be worth any trouble. Why don't we join the guys outside rather than stay here and argue about some guy."

"Alright, you win. But we'll still argue on this later." Elisa replied.

"No worries *pana*, I will always be here."

They all left her office and sat in the parlor. Most of the tattoo artists were busy working with their tattoo guns and needles. The room was poorly lit but there was extra lamps placed beside each customer's chair that gave more illumination to the artist. Isabella was very good at drawing tattoos and when her brother just got arrested, she had begun to help with drawing tattoos for customers. Now, she was taking a break from the job. She just got out of a bad relationship and it had affected her in every way so she was trying to take things slow till she began to feel good again.

"Why don't we all get new tattoos?"

"What?" she never realized she was lost in thought. She was not sure yet what she would do to get things back to normal in her life. She had thought that she could use work to keep her mind off it but the day she almost drilled into a customer's neck, she gave herself a break. Three months seems to be a very long time to get over a break up.

He had not wanted to go to the parlor but the gang had said he needed to go, they were no longer cool with the way the

Mexicans were getting away with everything they had done. They death of Jo' was still fresh in their minds although it's been more than a decade since the incidence occurred. The Reapers have always bore a grudge against them since then but they didn't want to disturb the little peace that existed. If any gang of the Aztec Nation tried to cross into their neighborhood, he would be the beginning of revenge but since they have all been staying in their hood, there had been no cause for trouble.

His father Tyrone Sr. was a close pal with Jo' and he had made him promise that the gang would not stop looking for a way to revenge the death of their brother and leader. Since Carlito's lock up, The Reapers have been looking for a way to strike a little blow that will incite the Mexicans to come attack them with full force then they would be able to have their revenge in full. He had been sent to go check out the Mexicans abode, to see where they could cause a little trouble that they wouldn't be able to let go. When he saw the tattoo parlor, he remembered that it was owned by Carlito but his baby sister was the one running it now. He went in to check it out, he had thought it would be their first stop when the gang decides to come into town but when he bumped into those girls at the entrance, and he had been having doubts of coming there.

He had seen Carlito's sister from a distance many times and he knew that she must be a beauty but seeing her stand right in front of him, he could hardly believe that such a creature as Isabella Sanchez could be related to Carlito. She was far prettier than he had imagined and her body, how he wished she was already naked on his bed. Her jeans also helped him appreciate the wonderful curve of her hips, how soft her booty would be. Her breast was not very large but it had a good posture, it looked soft and tender. That girl was something he could not walk by without having a taste of. He was sure he would be coming back for her soon.

****

*****

Isabella had just arrived at home, she had been thinking of going out to the club to hang out with her babes but she decided to stay at home instead. She could really use extra hours of sleep maybe that would help take her mind off Gomez. She thought of how she had spent her day. She had watched movies all morning till her friends showed up early in the afternoon and they hung out by the pool. She remembered Naty's guy, that's if you could call a guy you slept with five days ago and hasn't called you since then your guy. He was such a jackass; at least he could have been modest enough to talk to her. Now, she was not the only one trying to mend a broken heart, Naty had joined the team. She hoped that they would both get over it soon. Then her mind went to that guy they bumped into at the entrance to her parlor.

She had been trying not to think of him since she saw him. He had such a very cool dark eye that looked as if he could see into her barest soul. His voice was also soothing; all her worries had vanished when he spoke, it was like he gained control of her nerves and calmed all that was unsettled in her but one thing that didn't stop racing even after he left was her heart. She wished she could have followed him as he left but he was a total stranger.

Come to think of it, it was very unusual for a black to visit a tattoo parlor that is mainly for Mexicans, not just any Mexican, really bad ones. Didn't the guy know that or was he trying to look for trouble? She would have to ask her workers what the guy came to do in the parlor. Despite the danger she believed the guy could be in, she really wished he would come back. She had the longing to have him fill her up with his dick. She was sure that his dick would be just as big as his body his.

She had thought she would be able to sleep but the thought of the black guy had made that impossible, instead, she was feeling very hot, her face began to blush and she started having tickles on her feet. It looked like she would have to touch herself tonight. She had not had sex since she broke up with Gomez although she never thought she would remain single for this long. Her wet palms went up her bra and she gently rubbed against her breast. Soon, she was topless with her hands cupping her breast. She took her hard nipples in her mouth and gently sucked it. Her pants were getting wet but she wanted to be very ecstatic before she went down there. Her blood was rushing and the hotness on her face was greatly heightened. She was beginning to moan softly so she went down to her labella majora. She gently rubbed till it was getting too much for her to handle. Her fingers were soon inserted into her with her thumb rubbing the clitoris. All her live, she had never felt this sexually excited while masturbating. This had a very different kind of feeling to it. The heat kept rising and she kept going deeper until it looked like she was getting close to falling off the edge of the cliff. She didn't stop for that and in the end; the fall was the most perfect thing she ever felt. It was purely ecstatic, soothing, sexually invigorating and breathtaking.

She went to the bathroom to take a shower, that guy was really something. She had masturbated just because she thoughts of him after seeing him for less than two minutes. Her body ached all over, it seemed like it was because she had not had a really good banging in a while. Maybe if the guy never came back, his face could help her feel wild, she needed the excitement.

The water was warm and it calmed down a bit more. As the water ran down her chest down crossing over her vagina, she could not help but bend backward. Her hand went down again and her finger dug deep into her vagina. She gently pumped herself, taking in every emotion that was ignited in her body. She had thought she'd had enough but it seems she was just getting started. Her other hand went up to her breast, smooching herself lightly. Her tongue was constantly wetting her lips that were getting dry easily. Her ecstasy could not afford to plummet now; she was highly intoxicated that when she finally felt spent, she was breathless. The water was still running down her body while she was having a great moment alone, well not alone.

She rubbed the soap on her body and patiently had her shower. After one hour, she got out of the bathroom feeling terribly refreshed. She was very calm, her thoughts stayed only with the black guy that she had to see at whatever cost. She slept naked for the first time in a long time, letting the bed sheet keep her warm and sexually excited. No sooner had she jumped on the bed that she slept off. It was the most peaceful sleep she had enjoyed in months.

She dreamt of seeing the black guy in her parlor. They went into her office and there on the table, they made love to each other.

The ray of sun was streaking through the blind, beaming down on earth. Her face glistened as she lay on the bed. The time was just six minutes before seven and she hadn't stirred since she fell asleep. It was Thursday and she had fixed shopping for today with her friends. They weren't able to do any shopping the previous day so they shifted it. The breeze ruffled her blonde hair and the cold she felt on her face woke her up.

She looked at the golden morning that adorned the blue sky; it looked like it would be a beautiful day after a very great night. She laid on her bed for thirty more minutes, trying to figure out how she would spend her day. She would be going shopping with her friends by eleven that morning but after that she didn't know what else she would do. She didn't feel like going to Casa de la Tinta today, she felt like seeing the black guy again but she was not feeling up to it.

The bed seemed like it would not let her go. Her body no longer ached instead she felt very refreshed. How she wished she had known how to make herself feel this way a long time ago. Probably it was not her, it was her guy. She should go to the parlor today and find out something about him but she later decided not to. She had her bath carefully washing those parts of her body that helped her have a good night rest and in her panties but no top, she went to make herself breakfast. She prepared chilaquiles and fried egg then she drank her homemade pineapple juice.

She no longer felt like she should go out at all but she could not let her babes down, they have been clamoring for a time-out for long. She went back to her room and watched some mojo movies online. She could remember the last time she did that. She was still in high school and there was no guy approaching her, they were all afraid of her brother. She had used the movies then for masturbating but later she left that and was able to get excited all on her own.

It wasn't until past ten when she got bored with the movie that she noticed that there was noise coming from downstairs. It looked like her friends were around. She put on a blouse and went down to check.

It was just Natalia and Elisa who were around. They were going through the wine collection trying to decide which one to go for and without much hassle they settled for brandy since the shelve contained more of tequila and rum than any wine.

"You guys seem to have sorted yourselves out" Isabella commented.

"We thought you sleepy head would still be in bed." Elisa said. She walked away from the bar and sat on the divan settee, resting her back on the red pillows with black rectangular dots.

"I woke up early this morning." She answered.

Both friends looked at her with surprise. "How's that possible, you never wake up before ten." Naty said.

"She's just pulling our legs Naty, how can she wake up before ten? I have never seen that happen before." Elisa commented

"Can't I have a day that's just different from the way every other day has been for a long time?" she asked.

"Well, I guess you could have but something has to happen before there would be a chance of that happening." Elisa said.

"Maybe something did happen then. Why do you guys really care?" she asked.

"You mean something has happened and we don't know about it? We really care to know what's caused this big change in you." Naty said.

"Or maybe............" Elisa turned to Naty and then back at Isabella with her mouth agape. "Oh my God!........ This girl has been banged really hard. Can't you see the glimmer in her face?"

"*Hijole! Esas son mamadas!* How can you think that? Can I not have a normal day again?" she looked at her friends in the eye and then continued. "I didn't get banged by any guy yesterday night and if you girls do as much as whisper about this............" She left the statement unfinished not knowing what to say. She understood they were just surprised about the sudden change. But she thought to herself, that is what having a guy in your life could do. Just as she expected, they were not going to let her go easily. Naty was the one who spoke up now.

"If you are so sure that it's not a guy that got you all......worked up like this, why don't you then tell us? We would be happy to hear it and I am sure that we Vanessa would also have loved to hear it if she were here."

"Now I don't understand why you all must always mention my name in conversations." She strolled into the living room in her blue chiffon dress and light blue heeled sandal. She stopped for a moment and studied the three of them.

"*Que rollo con en hoyo.*" She looked around again when none of them was ready to talk. "Are you girls going to keep quiet or is someone going to tell me just what has been happening here before I walked in?"

Elisa and Naty gave Isabella the look that suggested that she had just started trouble today and she knew it.

"We think Isabella here made out with some guy yesterday night but she doesn't want to talk about it."

"And can you believe that Diamante here woke up early today, I mean she woke up before ten. Can you believe that?" Elisa added.

"No *mames!*" she exclaimed. She ran to Isabella and looked her over. "I can see that something is different in her today. Her face looks way calmer. I am very sure the guy must still be upstairs. Am I right?"

"You girls cannot frustrate me today." She stared at them for a while before she continued. "You know what? I would be spending the whole day at the parlor." She paused for them to get the idea. "Shopping has just been cancelled."

"No way, you can't do that." Naty exclaimed.

"You must be joking right?" Vanessa asked.

She looked at them with a smug on her face. That was the face she gave them whenever she was been serious.

"Does it look like I am playing around? I know you girls wouldn't want to go shopping without me so you are welcome to sit with me at the parlor."

"You just spoilt the day Diamante." Elisa said.

"You girls were not ready to stop strangling my neck. At least that would keep the leash on you babes for some days." She smiled at them and said.

"Let me get dressed so that we can be on our way."

"Dress up and don't come back Diamante." Naty shouted after her.

"Alright, I will just stay in bed with the big black guy then or.................." it was already out of her mouth before she realized what she said. Now she wouldn't be able to escape from their questions. They will make sure she spills everything that was in her.

"What did you just say Bella?" Vanessa shouted.

She didn't answer. There was no way she could avoid this. She was in for a whole lot of trouble.

"Hey Isabella, you'd better come down here and explain yourself. If you don't do that early now, you might not get the chance to get to your parlor." Vanessa said again.

She put on a plain white peasant blouse on blue denim shorts on her white banded George Crista Wedge sandals. She was going to the parlor today and nothing would stop her from going, even if she had to tell her friends all she did during the night.

She came down gently trying not to make any noise on the stairs but not quite surprising, they were all waiting for her, listening attentively for her arrival. She stopped midway and looked at them all posed waiting for her to come down and give them a very long gist about what she did in private.

"Seriously girls, why do you want me to go through all this?" she asked, looking for a way to avoid interrogation even though she knew it would fail.

Elisa spoke up. "You can be very sure that at this moment we are not leaving this house until we get the full gist of what happened from you."

Both Vanessa and Naty echoed their assent. "Si"

"Girls, I am going to tell you all about it. Just be patient with me." She replied.

"Ok. So what do you want to start with?" Vanessa asked.

"Maybe she should start by telling us which black guy she was referring to? You know."

"Seriously girls! Why I didn't mean to say that. That just slipped out of my mouth. Let us forget I said that."

"Well, well, well. Why shouldn't you tell us then why a black guy would come into your mind that your mouth would have had the opportunity to spit it out?" Naty asked.

"As I said before I don't know. It just came out." She lied again hoping they would get convinced and ignore that discussion.

"Wait a minute. You said a black guy right?"

"Yes, what is it?" she asked.

"Do you girls remember that guy from the parlor yesterday?" Vanessa asked.

"That black dude with those big stuffs?" Elisa asked.

"Yeah, that one."

"You guys seeing what I am seeing?" Vanessa asked.

"It is very visible now." Naty answered.

"But you said you were not into him yesterday? Where did you guys meet again?" Elisa asked.

"I said I wasn't with any guy yesterday and that's the truth. And I have not met the black guy we are talking about here." Isabella answered.

"Then why should it be that it is staying in bed with a black guy you met for how many minutes that should come to your mind when you are looking for a way to elude us. Something bigger is going on and you are not telling us about it. What is it Bella?" Naty asked.

"Ok, you girls got me. I like that guy but that's all there is about it. No big stuff." She looked at their victorious eyes widen with surprise.

"You like that guy? Well it's just normal. That guy is such a creature." Vanessa said.

"So hope we will still be going shopping?" Naty asked.

"No Naty. No shopping. I am going to the parlor now. I want to find out what that guy came to do in my parlor yesterday. It is unusual for black guys to come into old Carlito's property."

"Of course Diamante. You have found a new sport. I think you've had enough break. It is time you got a taste of a new guy." Elisa said.

"Whatever you girls say." She said with finality. It was her luck they loved what they heard first.

"So what did Pablo say?" Naty asked.

The moment they entered the parlor, her friends had become too chatty. They wouldn't let her do anything until she got all the information possible on the black guy. Pablo was the one she put in charge of her artist. He coordinated their work and every new customer was to go through him before they are assigned to any artist.

"He said his name is Tyrone." Isabella replied.

"Of course, he's a black guy. So how can you find him?" Naty asked.

"They said he dropped by this morning already, wanted to see me. So he'll be dropping by again late in the afternoon." Isabella answered.

"Oh my God! He's found you interesting already. Make sure you don't blow away this opportunity."

"Hey girls. I think he would be here to discuss business. I don't see him as one who would take the trouble of coming back here again just because he likes how my ass looks."

"Of course. Just don't forget to gist us after the meeting is over. I am sure something interesting would happen." Vanessa said.

"Ok girls. I would keep that in mind." She stood up from the edge of her table and went to sit behind her desk.

"Maybe we could do the shopping tomorrow." Isabella suggested.

"Are you kidding me? That's awesome." Elisa screamed.

"Well that's if you girls don't do something to fuck it up." She said.

"What! We won't even be around you." Vanessa answered.

"So you girls should go look for something good to do with your time."

They all left the tattoo parlor not yet sure of where they would go but they were currently satisfied that they would get an exclusive gist of whatever happens.

As fate would have it, as they were driving out of the parking lot, they saw a black guy that looked much like him drive in a 1996 Shelby. He looked just as attractive as he was yesterday. How was Isabella going to withstand having that before her and not fall beneath his knees, sucking his cock within minutes of seeing him?

He parked his Shelby and sat there for a moment. He knew he was taking the wrong decision but he also couldn't let this girl go. She had too much to offer that he would let it pass. He had called 2 Lasers and told him of the development. He was going to meet a woman today. He would pose as someone who was interested in opening a new business in the area. He didn't know what business he would be doing and that was why he was moving around. He had told them he would be back to the hood in two days.

He had to act fast. She must be his girl by the time he would leave.

He got out of his car and walked towards the parlor. He looked around and he noticed that there were more Azteca gang members than yesterday. He must have caught the attention of someone. He knew they won't strike him so he had to remain cool. The time to fight was near but not yet come.

He acknowledged their presence and walked into Casa de la Tinta. He went to meet the guy who told him to come back today.

"Er' my friend. I was here yesterday." He said.

"Of course, I remember you man. She's around; I'll tell her you're here."

The man walked to a door by the far right corner and after some seconds came back out.

"She'll see you in a moment. So if you don't mind, just take a seat."

He liked her style. He was sure she also knew already that something had to be wrong with him. How would he have walked into a Mexican only zone, maybe by mistake the first time, but still coming back again? They would both just have to play it out.

After two minutes, the big white-haired guy came to him and told him to go inside that she was ready to see him.

She had to visit the toilet to do a quickie on herself. The heat had returned when she heard that he was around. She was still unable to understand why she felt this way because of him. He was very attractive, strong and looks like he would be nice but that shouldn't cause her to keep having sexual urges whenever she saw him or thought of him. She composed herself for his entrance.

He pushed the door open and entered facing her. She was a mother fuck'n beauty. When she stood up to shake his hands, he had a good look at her leg. They were super sexy. Long, slim and fresh, just the way he loved it. He could see her cleavage and he imagined holding her breast in his hands. It would be totally mesmerizing when he fucks her.

"So I hear you are new in the area? How can I be of assistance?" she asked.

"I know that there are more professionals who can provide me with the information I want but from what I've gathered around, you seem to have been around for a long time and you definitely know how to manage things in the area." He said.

"Thanks for the compliment but it's just my parlor that I focus on. I don't have any kind of excellent business skill but I guess I am good at what I do." Her voice was still a bit shaky but she was beginning to gain composure.

"Ok. I don't think I want to waste your time much. I just laid my hands on some cash and I am looking to start a business with it. I thought of opening up the business down in South Main Street Broadway but I got a different idea." He paused and watched her for some split seconds and saw that she was paying very close attention to him so he continued.

"I thought of leaving home, try something risky and see what comes out of it. You know?" he said.

She decided that they could keep playing the different roles they felt comfortable to play or they could just man up and face the situation.

"You know Tyrone........ Or do you have a better name you want me to call you?" she asked.

"We can go around all day discussing the business you are never going to start or we can discuss why you are really here."

"I don't think I follow you." He said trying not to let go yet.

"I am sure you know this is a regular joint for the Mexican gang. What I don't understand is why you would still be willing to come back here a second time. What are you here for Tyrone?" she asked him again.

"Okay, you got me. Why am I here? That's gonna be a lil bit hard to talk about. I am sure that ya suspecting already that I aint no business guy." He stood up from the chair and pulled the drapes back a bit. He saw the guys have increased so he decided to play it cool.

"What do you say to hangin out with me; let's go have a drink right now anywhere you want. Its past six already, I am sure we can get an early drink. Then I would tell you everything you need to know." He proposed.

"So you some kind of street guy?" she asked.

"You could put it that way. But that's not the deal right now. I aint here to hurt you so be calm but I need you to get me outta here safely. Can you do that?" he asked her.

"I should be able to." She answered. "I hope you aint like some busta just looking to make some few cash off the streets." She asked him. She knew that even if he was, she'd still readily lay her ass open for him to do whatever he liked with it.

"No, you can chill as we walk out. I aint here for your paper." Under his breath he said. "I am here for something way better."

They both walked out of her office holding hands. She was laughing hysterically and he was all over her, caressing every part of her body his hand could reach.

They drove in their cars and raced towards E Beverly Boulevard to La Fiesta. The

Mexican crew had filled the parlor when they came out. Maybe the show she put on would make them cool down for a while.

Her body was like he'd thought it would be. Very cool, soft and tender and it could really use someone's hand like his.

There were few people in the bar so they took a secluded area to sit. As usual, she was served tequila with lime and he had the same thing she did.

"So why don't you begin to talk." She said.

"I am sorry but I can't remember you telling me your name. Don't you think that's kind of rude?" he teased.

"I don't believe you don't already know my name." she answered.

"And I am sure it aint gonna take nothing for you to tell me. You know just for formality." He smiled at her.

She smiled back. "Ok. I know your type. You want me to keep arguing with you over telling you my name then at last, you would get away without answering me what I asked." She looked at him with a "you see, you can't fool me look". "Isabella, that's my name."

"Of course. Only a pretty girl like you would have such a name."

"You can stop the flatter now. What are you doing here? It is not safe for you to be here and you know that right?" she asked.

"I know all that but why should I give a fuck about my safety when I can be parlayin with you all day." He said. Turning up the heat slowly.

"Of course, you could do that but you are not answering my questions." Isabella said.

"Let's do this bella. Let us forget about how safe I am and have fun. Let me worry about myself." He said.

"Ok. I could use some fun you know. I've been kind of stuck up for few months now." she said.

"What! How the fuck is that possible. You're fuckin hot. Don't they see that?" he asked.

"It's not dem guys, it's me. I broke up with my asshole boyfriend about two months ago."

"What'd he do?" he asked.

"I caught the fucker bangin some side chic of his. And he still got the guts to come to me and try to fuck me to." Her face was softened a bit. "You know, I really loved him and I thought he did too. I haven't got over him yet." She looked up at him and saw the concern on his face.

"Hey babe, I am sorry you had to go through all that. Some of us guys are just that way but the guy's a real jackass."

"But hey, hope you know you can't spend your whole life weeping on something that's supposed to make you hard. You know, you won't just fall for another guy like that. Make sure he's not an asshole before you let yourself fall."

"Wow. You are such an adviser. So what about you?" she asked the question that had been on her mind all day.

"What about me?" he asked.

"You know what I am asking. You got a girl?" she asked.

"Yeah, used to but not anymore. Not like your story though. She got hit by some blind mother fucker last year."

"I am sorry to hear that Tyrone. But hope you've had time to heal?"

"I am way past healing now babe." He answered.

"Then why does an attractive young man like you not have a girl also?" she asked.

"Let's just say I am looking for that girl who's just going to do right by me." He answered.

"Looking out for your future I guess. It's good though." She said.

The conversation was beginning to get personal and private. He was not looking for someone to pour his out to right now. He just needed someone to have something steady with not for a long time though.

"So how's it been for the past two months?" he asked.

"How's what been?" she asked not understanding what he was asking.

"I mean those guys you've had to put up with. You know, when you decide to have some fun." He offered.

"And who said I did any of that?" she replied.

"Well, I don't expect that you would have gone on sex break because your boyfriend broke your heart. At least once in a while, you would have come out to let out some heat." He answered.

"Sorry to disappoint you but I didn't. I guess I preferred to be on my own those times." She knew what he was trying to get at and that was somewhere that would be nice to end the talk and start the real deal.

"Wow, you are really surprising. So you mean for two months now, there has been no sexual activity for you? How did you manage that?"

"As you can see, I managed just fine."

"Well, you don't have to anymore. You can now have fun every time you feel like it."

"Why do you think you bangin me sound appealing to me?" she teased.

"Come on babe, I been seein the way you lookin at me, trippin all over me. I was just trying to be some cool dude. Let's cut the chase here and go to the real deal."

"And what would that be?" she asked smiling.

"I love your body. You got everything I am looking for. The nice tits, the slender legs, your hips are well carved. Your lips look like they would readily melt into my mouth so why shouldn't I be diggin you."

"I can see you really wish to have me but I aint interested." She answered.

"Come on love. You don't have to make me beg you before we do what we both want. I know you want me as much as I do you but you tryna make me crawl on ma knees aint gonna solve nothing."

"Come on Tyrone, do you mean to tell me you can't beg for the ass you'll be banging real hard soon?" Isabella teased.

"And are you gonna say all I've been doing aint enough work to get you?"

"Okay. Let me cut you some slack. You have tried a little bit, though not enough. So we go to my place?"

"Chill babe. We have all the night to ourselves. Why should rush it. Let us have more drinks here and when it's a bit darker, we'll leave for wherever seems appropriate."

"I love that idea." Isabella commented.

"So you wanna tell me about yourself?" Tyrone asked.

"Why do you want to do that? I thought we were not trying to get personal?" She said.

"Don't you think it would help to know a little about someone you'll be fucking frequently?" Tyrone asked.

"I didn't know we'll be doing this more than once. So you already believe that there would be a next time for us to have sex again?"

"I am sure I mentioned that I would be in your hood for a while looking for the right kind of business that will really pay."

"Maybe ass-fucking would sound as a good business to you I don't know." She teased. She never believed she could have this much fun with a guy this quick. She had thought she would still need about six months to be completely over Gomez but for the past one hour they'd been sitting and talking, no thoughts of Gomez or the mess her life was in came to her mind.

"You know, you're too good for me." She said.

"Why do you say that mia?" Tyrone asked.

"Hey what's the pity face for? I don't mean you as a dick man. I mean here, now, you've just been much fun." She said.

"Now you don't go on and give me all the credit. You are not a bad company either. It's also been long since I had a conversation like this." Tyrone said.

"I don't know why yet but I feel like it's dark enough. Can we leave now?" Isabella asked.

"I get the drill bella. We can leave for your place whenever you want to."

"Okay, let's go now." She had done her best and had been good for over one hour they were there. Her sexual urge had been heightened since he walked into her office. At least she didn't have to go beg him to fuck her before he gave the proposal.

Tyrone called the waiter and settled their bill. He didn't expect that he would be able to get her into bed today. Getting to sit with her and talk he had been able to see a different side of her. He had always reasoned that since she was Carlito's sister, she would be so power-conscious. But since he'd been with her, she'd been a great person to have a conversation with. He could only wish she'd be that good also in bed.

She said she didn't feel like driving home so they went in his car after she parked her car in a nearby underground garage.

His Shelby had brown leather upholstery that felt cool against her skin. She wished her beneath was in direct contact with the upholstery, maybe it would have done a little to cool the heat she could feel. She was getting nervous as they got closer to her house. It had been long since she had any guy penetrated her; she wondered if she'll remember how it feels. Yesterday night was a remembrance of al what she had missed and how great it felt. She knew that at the end, she would love it but she still felt nervous.

She directed him to her street and soon they were parked in front of her house. Tyrone came to her side of the car and opened the door for her to come down.

"Hope you enjoyed the ride?" Tyrone asked.

"It was great. Your seat was really comfy I must confess." She replied.

"You got a nice house here also." He commented.

"Thank you. I was thinking of selling it. When I bought five months ago, Gomez and I just moved in together then and not long after that he did that shitty stuff I told you about." Isabella said.

"I don't think I've ever heard of someone who has been such an asshole as this Gomez of a guy." Tyrone joked.

"So you want to come in? Or should we stay outside?" Isabella asked.

"No, let's go inside. I am sure there's a comfortable bed waiting for us."

"Wow, I would have such a great night." Isabella shouted.

"You bet you would." He walked through the hallway into the living room.

"This house is quite huge. How do you manage to stay alone?" Tyrone asked.

"I don't know. I guess I am a born loner." She answered.

"I am sorry but it seems I am little rusty with all these stuffs." He stopped and looked around the living room for a while.

"How am I supposed to start this? I don't want to spoil the moment at all." Tyrone said.

"I don't know, maybe you are just supposed to grab my ass and let your imagination guide you."

"That seems like a good idea but why don't we get something to drink. I feel like getting high a bit."

He looked around the house again. "Or do you by any chance keep some dope around?"

"What the fuck is wrong with you Tyrone! Maybe I shouldn't even get you that drink you need." Isabella said.

He rushed towards her and grabbed her from behind. Her skin felt good against his hand. She was soft and tender just like he imagined.

He turned her to face him. Her mouth was quivering and her whole body was shook gently. He pulled her close and planted a short kiss on her lips. He pulled back and looked at her face again. He could see the longing in her eyes. He gently returned his mouth to hers and kept kissing her deep.

The heat began to build up in her and he could feel it too. She felt his hand slide away from her neck and cupped her breast through her cloth. She shivered at his touch, it really felt good. She kissed him back when he tried to pull his lips away again.

He slowly felt his way through the top of the dress and down into her bra. Her naked flesh touched his hand and that sparked some emotion.

He cupped her naked breast in his hand and gently smooched her. Moans escaped from her mouth a little as he swallowed it up with another ravenous kiss.

Their clothes were off, they quietly moaned as they explored each other's body. He had carried her from the living room to the kitchen and then up to the bedroom. All the feelings she had forgotten she had were all rushing back. She totally forgot how much she loved foreplay. As he gently caressed her body, she felt herself being transformed into another realm. Her ecstasy was greatly heightened as he kept feeling her up. His hand worked wonders on her body, she was gently quivering beneath his touch. Whatever she felt yesterday was beginning to fade away. To have him do the real thing to her would be way better than she imagining it and doing it for herself.

He slipped his finger beneath her panties and slowly pulled it down. Her body quaked as his fingers grazed her clitoris. He would really do wonders to her tonight.

He came back to her vagina again and played with it. She gasped as his fingers found its way into her. He rubbed her inside, pulling it out and inserting it back. She was off the cliff already and they had not even tried to start the real deal.

He stood up from her side and let her catch her breath.

She was damn hot. He knew she would be great but no this great. He was sure she was still a bit dull after all her months of inactivity.

She was beginning to breathe less fast so he joined her back in bed. She was totally naked. Her body was very beautiful. Her breast was even fuller than he had imagined it would be and down there between her legs, it was very welcoming.

She came to him and kissed him. The kiss deepened little by little till they had to pause to catch little air. She pushed her hands towards his jean and unbelted it. She opened the zipper and down into his boxers she went.

Her skin felt really good. Even though she was hot from all what he'd been doing to her, her palms still managed to be cold. She slowly dragged the trousers down as she went below to his groin.

She pushed his dick into her mouth and gave it the best suck of its existence. She stopped now and then to suck his testicle sac and then went back to his penis.

Soon, they were almost spent. Tyrone pushed her back against the bed.

"Lay still." He told her.

He went between her legs again and with his tongue he licked her. She wondered if she wouldn't explode from all what he's been doing to her.

He left beneath her and came back to kissing her. As they kissed, he adjusted her hips till he was fully on top of her. Like a tornado hitting a small village, he went into her and she almost screamed at that instant.

"Oh my God!" she exclaimed. "How did you do that?" she asked.

"Guess I have a few tricks." He answered.

He slowly pumped her and she gave few gasps as it went on. It totally felt better to have the real thing in her.

His hand went down to her soft spot and he used that to keep rubbing the exposed part of her vagina. He was really going to get her full with sex. He increased the pace with which he came, he pumped her faster and she could not help herself again, she screamed out and kept screaming.

He came faster and faster and they both knew that at that moment they would both come.

When it finally did come, they were both too exhausted to say anything to each other. Tyrone never felt it was over cos he still wound his down to her again and kept rubbing her.

She would forever remember this guy even if they never had the opportunity to meet again.

He stood up from the bed and pulled her with him. They went to the bedroom and there bathed each other. Touching each other in between another quick round of hot sex they finally had enough.

They went to bed with Isabella cuddled against him. She recalled all the days she missed having that feel.

Definitely, it was good to have a guy in one's life.

The sun was almost at its peak when she woke up. She turned back to look at his sleepy face but no one was there. She went into the bathroom to check for him but he was not there either.

Well, it was late into the morning. He could have slipped away not wanting to disturb her.

It was really cool to have a guy go that length and please her.

She was really happy. Maybe she should go shopping with her friends today, that's if they want to. She can sit at home all day and just drown in the thoughts of when he would be back to make her feel this way again, probably even better. She had a quick shower and went back to bed.

Her tummy didn't give her worries about food and she was sincerely not dying to eat. She picked up her laptop and decided to research on him a little bit but she couldn't because all she knew was his first name. She knew that his former girlfriend's death would have passed silent. If he'd done anything to the guy who hit her he would have mentioned it yesterday. At least she had noticed that about him. He liked to brag about the things he did that were good.

Her phone rang and she prayed it was him but she remembered that she hadn't given him her number. She also cursed herself for not getting his. It was Naty calling her. Instinctively, she already knew what she would be asking about. She also knew that both Vanessa and Elisa would be there with her.

"Hey friend." Naty greeted her.

"Hey, sup?" She answered.

She could hear Naty telling Vanessa and Elisa how her voice was sounding so tired.

"Why do you sound tired Diamante. Didn't you have enough rest?" she asked as though she really cared if she rested well or not.

"Work was much at the parlor yesterday so I had to help them boys do a little of their work. You know, I think I need to hire some new set of tattoo artist to assist in making the job easier." She answered. She would not give them the satisfaction of getting all the information out of her so fast.

"You must be kidding me. So you have finally decided to call of your self-imposed strike uh?" Naty asked.

At least not all what she was going to tell them would be lies.

"I guess so. I just reasoned within me that why would I let someone else's action change the whole of my life and he is living very ok, unconcerned of what he did to me." She answered again, smiling to herself. It was not something she had not been thinking of. Almost every day, she wakes up and look at all that she had and wondered if she would ever get someone to share it with.

"Oh! That's very good. That means you would have little problem hanging out with that black guy, Tyrone right?" she asked.

"I never said I would have any problem hanging with him or anybody." She answered trying to sound offended.

She just continued as though she didn't hear the friendly contempt Isabella replied her with. "Wait" she said.

"Or was he able to make it yesterday?" Elisa shouted from the background.

She didn't really think she should lie about meeting him. She was already considering talking to them about everything. "Yeah, we did meet." She replied standoffishly.

"And how was he?" Vanessa asked.

"We talked about the business he wanted to start and where he should it." She answered.

"He also wants to start a business?" Elisa asked.

"Yes, why do you sound like that Elisa?" Isabella asked.

"Like what?" she retorted.

"You know exactly what I am talking about so just spill and tell what it's all about." She guessed she already knew what the answer would be.

"It's really worth nothing. I was just thinking that Henrique was also looking to start a business here and he did that terrible stuff to me. I was just thinking if that guy was also not like that you know." She answered.

"And why should I be worried if he happened to be like Henrique. Isn't it the girls he is going after you should be telling that to." Isabella answered trying hard to sound pissed.

"Come on Diamante, I just thought that you and the guy would have done some other stuff apart from business."

She decided to come clean. "Well we did do stuffs away from business." She said. They were all shouting at her to tell them what happened.

"I only said we did other things apart from business and you girls are this eager to hear what I have to say."

"Don't you even think that maybe it could be something boring?" she asked.

"Was it something boring?" they asked in unison.

"No." she answered.

"In fact, it was a very fun stuff we did. We had sex!" She exclaimed.

"Like I knew it" Elisa cried out.

"How was it?" They asked her again.

"It was very great." She answered,

She kept going into details all what they did the previous night.

****
*****

He drove his car into his driveway. It had been days since he'd slept on his own bed and he really missed it. The traffic was getting worse these days. He had spent almost half the time for the journey in the traffic he was in.

He wished he had said goodbye to her but it was better this way. He didn't want things to be too complicated when they go over to her hood and destroy what they could see of which he was sure her tattoo parlor would be among. She smiled while she slept. Her lips were lightly parted and he dropped a kiss on her mouth, she had licked it when he did it.

Before it was dawn, he had left her house and within thirty minutes, he was on his way to South downtown L.A.

His crew had called him that morning and told him that they needed him at home. They wouldn't tell him why he was needed at home at such a time. He never really minded their call, if they hadn't called, it would have been almost impossible for him to leave her. When Little Jack, his lil bro called him, he sounded kind of scared. Maybe something bad happened while he was away. He pressed him to say what was wrong but he wouldn't bulge. His brother Jeremy was the only family he had left alive and he couldn't do anything that would endanger him. He was a boy and still looked up to him a great deal. He couldn't let anything happen to him. His brother would always be his first priority, then himself, then the gang can follow.

He wasn't sure yet how he'd tell them his visit to the forbidden hood was. He would try to look for a way to make sure that he went back.

His homies on the street would expect him to have a plan ready. Few days ago, he had thought he had but now, he wasn't sure if he would be able to follow that through. They always meet minutes before noon. He checked his watch and it was past eleven already. He had to come up with an idea and he had to do that fast.

As much as he loved to go back to the junk in the trunk, there were family stuffs to take care of. He donned his kicks and stuffed some kraft singles in his pocket.

The few days he had spent away from home, he had almost forgotten how nice it was hangin out with his real g's. He had not put his car in the garage yet so he drove away from the house fast.

When his brother called in the morning, he had told him to join them in the meeting. He would normally not let his younger bro be there as they were always at the risk of getting caught by the cops. That was where all their deals were discussed before he finalizes them on his own.

He turned off Hooper Ave. into East Washington Boulevard. He bought his house in Compton Avenue five years ago after staying for three years in his father's house after his death. It was a three bedroom semi-detached house. They had a backyard lawn where they played basketball with their friends when they were young. The memories he had there were mostly good ones but he had some few very terrible ones.

He could remember when his mother was murdered in the house. His father had taken them to an uncle that stayed in Compton then till the police finished their investigation. He had told them nothing after the incident but when he finished high school and got admission into college, he told him what really happened. A guy named Felipe had ordered that his father be dealt with. But he and the other gang had a client who had tried to talk to the Feds so they had gone to deal with him that night. When the hit men came, they met only their mother at home and they killed her.

He knew that even if he decides not to go heads on with the Aztec Nation because of Jo', he would definitely do it for his mama.

As he neared their meeting point, he looked around to see if the cops were around. They were not doing dope today, just guns they needed for a hit that they just got information on.

The other guys had arrived before he got there. The house was an abandoned warehouse his father purchased two months before he died. He had just got a job to sell out some government-issued black market firearms. When he died, he had turned it to their meeting point and for a long time now, it had served them well. The cops frequented the place but they had some cops in their pocket so they were never around whenever a raid was to be carried out.

Pope, Fleeker, Breezy, Duncan, Old guy and Jerry were waiting at the entrance to the warehouse. He was the only one who had a key to the place so that they wouldn't have to mess it up when he wasn't around. They had a different joint for flexing, chilling and partying.

"Hey homies, how ya'll doing?" he asked.

"Cool man. How's the other side?" Old guy asked. They called the Mexican's hood the other side. "It looked dope bro but I don't think it will remain that way for long." He replied.

"Seems like ya gat where we'd be hittin dem motherfuckers hard." Pope said.

"I ain't sure I'm done with that yet. I gotta skip town again. Looks like there might'a been some things I didn't take notice of." Tyrone answered.

"So what the stuff ya were saying over the phone this morning?" he asked his brother who had remained throughout the conversation.

"It's bout dem Mexicans Tyrone. We been hearing they got some kinda big stuff about to happen." He answered.

"I don't grab what you saying." He said looking confused.

"We hear they know that you been rolling around their hood. Going places where nobody been send you to." He explained.

"Okay, so they know I am in town, they didn't come for me. Why is that?" he asked.

"They say it's because you been banging one of their fly chics." He continued.

"I expect you niggers to understand that I am the boss here and I know what I am doing. If I bang one girl or anyone, maybe I was just deciding to have some fun." He replied.

"I aint against you having some time to chill out and sample some of their products but ya know what's at stake here bro. We all are expecting to deal with dem assholes once and for all." Jerry answered.

"Hey brothers, let's forget about what ama need to do over there. I can handle myself." He said.

They entered the warehouse to discuss the main issue of the day. While he was away, a new shipment of guns had arrived and their contact guy said he needed a raise. The cash he had left to cover the deal was not enough so they had told him to come back in two days.

"How much raise is the punk asking for?" he asked.

"Thirty-percent" Fleeker answered.

"Who the fuck does that idiot think he is to ask for that? We are done with him. Pope you gotta take care of him tonight." Tyrone answered.

"Aight boss." He answered.

"So what else we gotta discuss before I bounce again. I gotta leave before nightfall." He said.

"We've really got to sit down and talk about how you handle yourself over there Tyrone." Duncan said.

"Are you niggers serious about this shit?" he asked looking perplexed.

"I can fucking take care of myself." He said.

"Tyrone, it's just gonna be you against God knows how many Aztec people. How will you fucking take care of yourself then?" Breezy asked.

"So what you smart asses suggesting? I should stay put in my crib?" he asked.

"Come on, Shotz, that's preposterous man. We understand that you got the ghetto to protect but you aint gon be able to do that if ya dead. We just saying you should find a way to remain low key." Breezy answered.

"Then we are cool. I am gonna be in my base so if you need me ya'll know where to find me." He looked round at them before he continued. "And I'll be leaving for the other side in two days. I just remembered some things I gotta take care of."

"What's that Tyrone?" Old guy asked.

"You don't need to know any deets about it man. You be cool and tell Mrs. I said hello okay?" he said.

"Ok man. Just watch your back." He replied.

He walked out through the backdoor to wait for Jeremy. He didn't really say what was wrong. Jerry knew better than to worry about how he would take care of himself.

He was leaving the bunker in his house where he stashed his dope, money and guns. He went to select some guns he would be taking when he was leaving for the other end of L.A. the next day. After the meeting, he and his lil bro had a very long talk. It was not just that the Mexicans were aware he was around; they were also planning to hit them. There had been a major activity going on in their hideout. Their informant had told them that they just ordered to replenish their ammo store. They bought new knifes, guns and even bulletproof vests. He said something was going to happen soon but he didn't know whom they would be hitting yet.

He said they had been having problems with an Italian mob that were just trying to move into their locale. It could be those guys there were trying to take down or it could be The Reapers. He called them so that they could be prepared.

He knew that when he gets back there, it was to do real work. He might not have time to meet his fine-assed lady. He had to know what was going to happen, when it was going to happen and whom they would be hitting. He had told Jerry he would call him to give the news to him if they would be the one they would be attacking so that he could inform the remaining members of the gang so they could be at alert always.

He had called Pope next and told him to delay the assignment he gave him. He sent the money to settle the thirty percent their guy asked for. The guns were already on the way and they were sure it would arrive in lesser than three days. He would have waited for it before he left for his new home but he wanted to see if he could bang Isabella again before he disappeared.

He did not have any idea how he would go about getting the information he needed. He didn't want to endanger the life of their informant by making him keep feeding them info. They would find out soon enough and that could get him killed. He could still be useful later in the nearest future.

It was evening already and the next day he would leave. His brother had wanted to see him before he left but he wouldn't allow him. He knew that he might not get to come back when he goes this time.

He had sincerely wished he could make things work out for him and Isabella but the risks were too much. Her brother used to be a leader of the gang he was trying to take down now. He thought back to when he met her and then reasoned if he had not been compromised. She seemed to be a good girl and getting her involved in this gang stuff might not be good for her. He could remember seeing her playing around when he and his father came for a meeting years back. It was like she was oblivious of what was happening in her family.

Right now, she was grown and he was sure she understood how everything worked. He could decide to tell her and see what happens at last.

Morning soon crept into reality. He had woken up way before dawn. He went for a quick run, did some other cardio-exercises and push-ups. He was not up for any workout this morning so he just did little warm-up exercises.

He revved his car engine in the garage, pressed the button and the garage door opened. He backed his way out of the garage, wondering if he would ever get the opportunity to do this again. He made his way through the curvy intersection up to Santa Monica Freeway. He gladly journeyed back to his destination which could as well become the last he would be getting to.

Whatever the fuck could have happened to him? It's been three days since he left and she had asked around for his contact but it was all to no avail. She knew he would have the access to contact her but maybe he was just like Henrique. It would be disastrous if it turned out that he was just a player like Henrique. But how would he all because of getting between her legs, go through such trouble? It would probably be that something came up and he had to leave town.

That morning after talking with her friends, they had gone out to the mall and did a great deal of shopping. She upgraded her collection of ice. She had been eyeing one of those that have been on display for weeks now hoping it would still be available when she decided to shop.

When Vanessa, Naty and Elisa got to her house that morning, they ran up to her room shouting.

"Where the hell did you keep him?" Naty asked.

"Where did you guys do it?" Elisa asked.

"Hey girls, chill out." She looked at their eager faces waiting for her to say something about last night.

"Now Diamante, you will no longer be allowed to keep information about all these things to yourself. You would have to tell us everything that happened if you want us to be your friend." Vanessa said, looking very serious. Whenever Vanessa looked serious, then she was serious.

"Okay ladies, I would tell you what happened." She sat down on the bed and explained it all to them. Everything, from the parlor to the bar and till they got home, she gave them all the details.

"Wow!" Naty exclaimed.

"You guys were so hot. In how many hours did all this happen?" Elisa asked.

"All what? From the time we were in the office to the time we spent at the bar? Or what are you asking?" she asked.

"You know what I am asking Isabella. How long did that guy last on you?" Elisa asked again.

"Well, I get you now, he lasted for too long I must tell you that. I was beginning to think that I would have to beg him to stop but he kinda seemed to notice." She said.

"Is he that good?" Naty asked with mouths agape.

"If you want to know, why don't you try him out." She answered.

"Do you mean that? Like seriously mean what you just said?" Naty asked.

"What do you think? Do I joke with such matters?" Isabella asked, smiling deviously.

"And I was here thinking he could just be like Henrique you know. That guy who slept with you and dumped your ass. Yet you still want to sleep with this guy?" Isabella asked knowing that she was going to offend Naty soon.

"I made a mistake thinking that Henrique felt something special for me but I am not looking for anything special with Tyrone, I just want to have a taste of him." Naty replied.

"Okay, you are my friend and I wouldn't want to give you any hopes that he would be interested in you." When she saw Naty's countenance changing, she quickly added. "Not that he won't find you attractive, but from what he told me yesterday he is not into banging every girl he comes across and like."

"And he banged you?" Elisa asked.

"I think I have told you guys all about that. He did." Isabella answered.

"Then this guy must have a thing for you. He really did you well. Not just the quick sex but he was very patient with you." Vanessa said.

"Maybe he does, maybe I just know how to handle guys like him." Isabella answered.

"How many guys have you handled in all of your lifetime?" Naty asked.

"You expect me to slut around like you do Naty?" Isabella asked.

"Whatever." She decided to stop arguing and let the matter be.

"So has he called you yet?" Elisa asked.

"And why should you be concerned with when last I conversed with him? I have given you girls more than any of you would give me so be satisfied with that and don't bother me again." Isabella said and she knew that they wouldn't disturb her again.

"So are we still going out today?" Vanessa asked.

"I called you so that we could go out together. Do you think I would let that go because of some argument over some guy? You girls should give me a minute to change and we can be on our way."

It's been two days since all that happened and right now, she was no longer sure, the Tyrone really liked her. She had done the interview for the new tattoo artists yesterday. That had taken all her day and she was too tired to do anything when she got back home.

Waking up this morning and not still getting any call from him was no longer feeling cool.

She had to look for a way to get across to him. Even if it turns out that he was also an asshole, she would be able to move on with her life. She wouldn't let another guy make her life miserable again.

She had taken her bath and was ready to go her parlor. She looked out through the transparent glass on the hallway door and saw that there was a parked car in front of her house.

Her neighborhood was not one that had many of that so it was strange for her to see such. Just at the moment she was opening the door, there was a knock on the door that disappeared leaving only a resounding echo.

Tyrone was almost toppled when he tried to knock the door and the door was opened. He quickly regained his balance before he could fall down.

1

0

She stood there by the door looking at him. She didn't know what she was feeling on her inside. She wasn't really expecting to see him but she was glad he was here. At least it has proven that he was not an asshole and she was not going to have to go through what she did with Gomez.

"Are you going to say anything or do you want to keep staring at me all day?" Tyrone asked.

"Oh! I am sorry Tyrone. How are you?" she asked.

He was looking kind of different. All the times she had seen him he was wearing very cool t-shirts on either jeans or chinos trousers but today, he was wearing a black tailored-suit that would worth nothing less than three thousand grand. His whole look today was very businesslike. Maybe that was why he had not been able to contact her, he was dealing with business stuffs.

"I see that you have started real business research."

"Oh! Cos of the suit? It has nothing to do with business, I just felt like dressing up today."

Well, maybe she was wrong then but why is he here? "I never heard from you since that night." She said.

"I am sorry, I had to leave town for a few days to settle some stuffs at home." He explained.

"Oh! And hope everything is better now?" she asked.

"Well, we are working towards that. You know brother problem and the likes."

"Of course, I totally understand." She answered. She had feared that he would tell her that he was married and wouldn't be able to see her any longer.

"So what brings you here today? This early in the morning if you understand what I mean?" she asked.

"I was thinking about the other night and then I disappeared for some days so I thought I should come and explain to you what happened so that you don't begin to have funny ideas about what could have happened." He replied.

"But that's not the only reason I am here." As he said this, she saw it written all over his face that it was not going to be something good.

"And what's that?" she asked.

"I don't think it would be appropriate for me to say it here. So what do you say to dinner tonight, at my place?" He asked.

"Ok. I can work with that." She answered.

"So I'll come pick you up from the parlor at six thirty?" he asked.

"Yes you should. Don't come with your car, you'll drive mine." She said.

"Thought you said you loved my ride?" he asked.

"I love it but I didn't want to have to worry about my car. You'll drive me to your house in my car and I'll drive myself home, it's that simple." She said.

"Alright then, I won't come with my ride." He assented.

"What do you love to eat? Maybe I can get something very interesting for you." He asked.

"I eat anything and everything so don't worry about what I would love. I would love anything as long as you cook it well." She joked.

"Okay then, let me leave you to get to your work, I have delayed you enough." He moved away from the door to let her step out and lock the door.

At that moment, his eye went down to her buttocks. It was well shaped in the frock she wore. He wrapped his hands around her waist and grabbed her by the butt. She jerked a bit but settled later. She turned to him and they stood there kissing each other passionately. He was the one who broke the kiss.

"You should get to work now." he said.

As they turned to walk towards their cars, they saw the three ladies standing by the driveway staring at them. Isabella knew she was in for another round of questioning. As they walked towards her, she began to fear how she was going to introduce him to them.

"Hey girls, I am sure you've all met Tyrone before." Thank God that came to her mind.

"Hello Tyrone. I've been longing to see you after that great encounter." Elisa said.

"Thank you. I know you pretty ladies are all here to talk with your friend so I'll just leave you girls to talk." He said.

"Don't forget tonight." He whispered to her ear.

She nodded as he made his way to his car. They all had their eyes following his every step. After he drove away, they turned to Isabella.

Elisa asked. "How did you manage to get hold of this guy in just a few days?"

"That's not even what surprises me most. It was Isabella who was last to agree that this guy would be very good boyfriend material but see her now, she is the one getting the guy." Vanessa said.

"Please ladies; let's be on our way now. I need to pick which five guys from those I interviewed for the job yesterday and I am sure it's not going to be an easy job."

They all decided to let this one slip. They followed her to her car and she sped away to the parlor to begin her moment of deep imagination.

She was trying to pick the last person out of all those she had interviewed but it was almost impossible. She tried and blocked the thoughts of his hand on her hips, his mouth on her lips when she started and it worked but as she got closer to getting the job done, she could no longer mange to keep him out of her mind.

Seeing him again and feeling his hand one her made her remember the moment they shared. It was the greatest sexual moment of her life. She could still feel his hands on her hips, holding her tight, reviving the feeling that she had when he grabbed her the other night.

She had picked a guy named Pablo who was working in a smaller tattoo shop; she liked to have people with same name working under her. He brought some of his previous works and they were very great. She had known she would pick him once he left her office. She had also picked a Hernandez who also worked in a tattoo shop four years ago but since then he had been a local salesman. She also picked two guys who just got into the area. She was torn between choosing a Hispanic blonde guy whose father just died and was a pretty decent artist and an American who was just starting but seems to have much enthusiasm for the job.

She finally gave up. She called Pablo to help her select between two files that she placed on the table. They had no label showing whose own was which. He selected one and when she opened it, she saw that it was the American guy, Jones that got picked. She called everyone that she picked and told them to resume work as early as the next morning. They would all be on probation for two weeks. If they didn't do good jobs, they would have to lose the job.

If they passed and excelled during their probation period, they would join her team of thirty artists. All her artists were very loyal and they all had different ways and skill of designing. Every day, over a hundred clients come to do something about tattoo. They never closed the shop, they had different shifts and they all did their job well.

By the time she was through with the rigorous selection of her new employees, she went to have lunch. Naty was waiting at the lobby of her parlor. She had been working on her fashion blog since they arrived.

Vanessa and Elisa had gone to interview a lawyer for the new podcast they were about to release. They had been gone for almost two hours, which meant they would be through soon and would join them at lunch.

"Hey Naty, let's go." Isabella said.

"Okay, just give me a minute to post this. You know, I have been working to get the SEO in this article right. The last article didn't do well and I am guessing it was because I rushed the keyword research." Naty said.

"You know I don't understand a word of everything you've been saying. Just do what you have to do and let's be on our way." Isabella replied.

She closed the laptop and placed it in her bag. "I am done, so let's go."

They crossed the road and walked down the street till they came to the end of the block. The restaurant they frequented was just fifteen minutes away from the parlor. They were not interested in talking so they walked on in silence. They looked through the windows of stores as they walked on. Different antiques were always on display on this street. She had once bought a cup that was over two hundred and fifty years old as a present to Gomez and remembering it now, she thought she should buy something for Tyrone.

She was still unsure as to why he had asked her to come to dinner. It looked like things were not good and things would not remain good for long. It looked like he was giving her a goodbye when they had hardly welcomed each other. They had their first sex on their first date and she was sure that there was a high probability that would make love again tonight and it would be their last sex together.

They arrived at the restaurant soon enough. Vanessa and Elisa were already there waiting for them. "You guys are late, this is past two." Elisa said.

"Sorry, we both had to complete what we were doing." Naty replied.

They ordered for their meal and while they ate, they talked about the lawyer Elisa and Vanessa went to interview.

He was a graduate of Harvard, worked for a private firm, was married with two kids and had the ambition of starting his own firm soon. They interviewed about his take on life in East Los Angeles. They had discussed about why he moved to downtown L.A. to start a life. He had met his wife in a party his boss invited him to. She was American but she had lived all her life with Mexicans so she considered herself Mexican.

They chatted about what they interviewed him on and when they were leaving he had given them his number and told them to call him later in the week that he had something very cool for them to see. They all understood what that meant. He wanted to fuck them. They talked about how they went back immediately and told him that they could not wait to see what he had for them so he should them right now.

Right there in his office, they had a threesome that was spectacular. The guy had a very huge dick but he couldn't keep it standing for long. They covered for that when they touched each other for him. By the time they left his office, he was assuring them that he would divorce his wife just so that he could get to always do this with them.

Soon, they made their way back to the parlor together and gist all through the afternoon till evening. By the time Tyrone came to pick her up, they were all up to date about what was happening in each of their lives.

As he pulled her car out of the parking lot, she placed her hand over his hand that held the gear. He stopped and looked at her. She bent forward and kissed him for some seconds.

"What was that for?" he asked.

"Nothing. I have just been thinking of doing that for a long time so I just wanted to get it done." She answered.

"I never got the chance to ask but where do you stay?" she asked.

"Where do you think?" he asked her.

"How am I supposed to know? I don't expect that you would be staying in a hotel or guest house and have the opportunity to cook for me. Or am I wrong?" she asked.

"You are absolutely right" he said. "Well, I have an apartment kind of away from all the hustle and bustle of the town." He answered.

"So you are trying to tell me you like a quiet life. But I don't see that in you at all." She commented.

"Maybe that's because I have not been totally telling you the truth Isabella." He had said it at last. Now, anywhere they ended up this night, he was fine with it.

"What do you mean by that Tyrone?" she asked.

"Maybe we should start from, I am not just Tyrone, my niggers also call me 9 Shotz." He said.

"You are 9 Shotz?" she asked shocked. She had heard of 9 Shotz before. He was the guy who was in charge of The Reapers, a black gang that had been keeping a grudge against the Mexican gang Aztec Nation. It was the bloody war against each other that had resulted in the death of her parents. Since then Carlito had determined that he would do everything he could to make sure that he had his revenge. That was what made Carlito become the leader of the gang and what now makes him a prisoner, what was she to do?

"Are you fucking around with me or are you being serious she asked him." She knew he couldn't be joking with such stuff.

"I am serious bella. I just didn't know how to tell you earlier." He said.

She didn't know why but she believed him. She couldn't explain it but she felt like being with him more. She knew he was an enemy but she couldn't bring herself to hate him. She had felt what she felt for no one since she had started going into relationships and she was not about to let go of that. She looked at his face and saw that he was also confused. She knew this would be harder for him than it was for her. He was the leader of a gang that wanted her own people dead. She was the sister of his no one enemy yet he was trying to please her in all ways.

"Why did you come here then Tyrone?" she asked.

"To be honest, I was here to find out which location it would be best to hit you guys best so that you people can get pissed off and start a war with us." He answered.

"Now I know understand what's been happening." She said.

"What do you mean by that?" Tyrone asked.

"I shouldn't be talking to you about this. This could get my people killed." She said. She looked out of the window, darkness was beginning to descend. They had only been driving for what? Fifteen minutes? Yet it seemed like they had been on the road all day.

"I understand you." He looked at her face and saw how confused she was. She was in the middle of a fight that she knows nothing about and the little she knew she has no idea what it means.

"I actually went home to solve a family problem. My brother got wind of rumors that your people were preparing for a very big fight. Now we have not done anything that can cause them to prepare in such a way so we think the may be trying to prepare for a fight against the Italian mobs that just moved in to the other end of the city. " He looked at her; she seemed lost in her thoughts.

"You listening Bella?" he asked.

"Yeah, I am." She answered.

"Okay, I don't know why but I just feel like telling you everything so that you can understand what I am doing and why I am doing it."

"When I came here, the first time, I discovered that the best place for us to hit would be the tattoo parlor." He knew she'd react to this so he waited.

"What the fuck did you just say? Casa de la Tinta, you were going to destroy it? What are you?" she exclaimed looking at him with detest.

"I know that it is very horrible. But I didn't know this till I met you. I got to know that we don't have fight just because some people got killed some years ago." He said.

"I don't think you can say that because the only reason my brother is in prison is because he was the leader of Azteca which meant he had to be the one to do the killings, all of them. And this only happened because he was looking for a way to mete out his revenge on the black gang for the death of our parents. It was during this war they were killed and they were not even members of any gang."

"I am sorry to hear about that Isabella but I also lost my mother but not even in the war, in a more tragic way. She was murdered in our house while we were asleep in the adjacent room. We never knew until the next morning when my father arrived from an operation." He saw the terrified look she had on her face.

"So when I say I know that deciding not to stop the fight is not the best thing, I know what I am saying." He looked at her to see that she was calming down.

"I didn't want you to get involved in all this. I just wanted to give you a very good last night and disappear from your life forever. I don't mean any harm to you or the parlor. I have told them back at home that I haven't found any place we could hit yet."

"I am sorry I doubted you Tyrone." She said.

"It's okay. I understand the situation you are in." He answered. He turned the car into his driveway and parked by the door to his garage.

1

1

He came to her side of the door and opened it for her. She looked round the house; it was looking nice, at least for a guy of his reputation. She did not expect him to have time to take care of the house or even care what the house looked like.

He took her into the five bedroom detached house. Its living room was very wide and housed various kinds of chairs that she was sure no one had sat on. He had not even said how he got the house. She remembered how he had also dodged answering any question the first time they went out together. He was very good.

She sat down on one of the love seats. It was creamy in color and the silky clothing that was used to cover it was really nice.

"So your dad owned the house or what?" she asked.

"No. You really don't know when to back down Isabella." He said.

"This is the second time you are calling me Isabella tonight Tyrone or should I say 9 Shotz." She joked.

"No, my dad didn't will it to me, I killed the family that stayed there five days ago and I have been staying here on my own since then." He also joked.

"I see. And where did you keep their body?" she asked.

"I am very smart so I didn't dump their body anywhere. I actually bathed them with lye." He said.

"Wow. Why am I not frightened you would do the same to me?" she asked.

"Maybe it's because you know that I would be too tired to lift anything. I would have used all of me to please you so how would I have that energy." He said.

"You sure got a sweet mouth Tyrone." Isabella said. "So what are you serving me tonight?" she asked.

"What do you think? Were you really expecting that I would cook? I haven't cooked in years and if I try to do it, the result would be disastrous. So please don't expect any food." He said, raising his hands up to show that he was all she's got.

"Okay then. So what are we going to do all night? Or are we going to sit looking at each other?" she asked.

He walked back into the kitchen and came back with three big plates. He went back and came with two bottles of martini and two glasses. He opened the plate he had brought in. Two roasted chicken sat on each plate, blazing red and steaming hot.

"How did you know?" she asked.

"Know what?" he asked.

"That I love roasted chicken." She answered.

"Who said I knew. I just felt like eating roasted chicken and I decided I should share it with you." He answered.

"Am serious Tyrone, how did you know?" she asked again.

"I don't know if you can remember but my father and I came to a meeting that was to be headed by your brother. He was supposed to take you out for lunch but the meeting was an urgent one so he cancelled without telling you. In your rage you barged into the meeting and cried out *why are you trying to make me miss the roasted chicken, you're so mean.* I really thought it was funny then. But after your brother took you out of the room and came back inside, he said that you could die just to get a bite of roasted chicken. I don't know how but after I left your place this morning, I remembered what your brother said and I decided to surprise you." He explained.

"Oh my God! You are a darling." She dragged him down to her and gave him a big kiss.

"I think I would have to roast more chickens for you just so I can get that always." He said.

"You better not hope I would give you that the next time you make me roasted chicken." She said.

They feasted on the chicken talking about happy childhood memories. They talked about friends they had, what prep school was like, their first sex experience in high school and what party they attended in college.

Before they knew what they were doing, they had finished all the plates of chicken and the two bottles of martini. Tyrone got an extra two bottles for them and they kept drinking.

They were deep in their discussion when Isabella stood up and sat on Tyrone's lap.

She pushed her head towards his face and kissed him. He let her do it all. She explored the deeper parts of his mouth with her tongue and gently stroked the side of his mouth. He let her down his lap and laid her on the cushion. His hand crept up from beneath her frock up to her waist. She was still calm and desperately wanted to remain so throughout this great moment she was about to experience.

His hand moved out of the frock and the kiss deepened. He used his other hand to cup one of her breast in his hand. He gently pressed and massaged it with his finger. It felt like he had not touched her breast ever before. Her soft and tender skin felt warm and tingling to his palm. He continued pressing her and she was beginning to feel it coming. His other hand went back under her frock. He raised her hips slightly to give him the chance to everything he wanted. He slid her panties to one side and he rubbed his finger against her. She was wet already. He decided not to waste much time so with two of his fingers he dipped his hands into her. She felt the huge rush of emotion surge through her body. She exhaled after it passed. She wanted to remain calm tonight but it looked like when you are dealing with Tyrone, you could never be calm. His finger was pumping through her faster than the last time, it looked like she would come early today but just as he did the last time, he pulled his hand out of her again.

He went back to kissing her. He kissed every part of her body causing her to shiver uncontrollably. Soon, his trousers was down and she was out of her frock and just at that moment, his phone rang, he ignored it.

As he returned to kissing her, Isabella's phone also rang and simultaneously their phones kept ringing. They finally had to pick their calls.

As they received the news of what was about to happen, they stood there in shock.

What they heard would happen was not so good. They looked at each other and realized that they had both brought this upon their people. If they had not continued in their relationship maybe what was about to happen would not have been a probability, they were not just sure of what was going on any longer.

"What did they tell you Bella?" Tyrone asked her.

"What they told you I guess, my people are here and they need to take you with them."

"Well that would be hard I must say. My people also happen to be in the area. They wanted me to know that they have the city and only need an order from me. They said if I chicken out on them, they'll forget they have a leader and do what's necessary." He said.

They looked at each other, still naked with people ready to kill because of something they want. Isabella had known that the gang didn't approve of her sleeping with Tyrone but they also thought that she needed something to get her head back in the game and maybe that would be getting banged again even if it were to be by a black guy whom they wished they could have killed over and over again.

"What are we going to do Tyrone?" she asked him.

"I am very confused. I didn't finish some parts of the story I told you. My brother told me that if I fucked up because if the lady I'm banging then he would make sure that the gang knows it has no leader and that means they can do anything they really want in their heart."

"And you didn't think to tell me this? That just because you didn't think it would be good to destroy my people, your brother does not care how many people he destroys. You think that's not necessary?" she asked him, extremely pissed.

"I am sorry bella but I never thought anyone would be attacking anyone tonight. I thought I would have time to make my brother see that killing won't bring us peace from the death of my mother." He looked at her pacing back her forth with her breast slowly bouncing as she breathed.

"Bella, I am sorry. I would find a way to get us out of this I promise."

"Of course, I know that you would get us out of the situation. Don't you see that the only way for us to get out is for you to die and though I don't know how to define what I have for you, I am not ready to lose it so we are staying in here together."

They were both about to sit down when their phones rang again.

"Hey bro what's happening out there?" he asked.

"No, you don't have to do nothing. I am looking for a way to do it right, trust me man. We don't have to be the first to attack. What we need is someone to attack and make it look like we did. You dig? Then when they bring it to us, we use our upgraded firearms against them and by the time we are done with them, they would not realize we have just hit them. Let me handle this please." He looked at Isabella where she was and noticed that she was in a heated argument also.

"I know what I am saying Jeremy, you just need to trust me......... Oh! Thanks man, I won't let you down I swear it to you."

He waited for her to finish her call. When she finally did, her face was downcast.

"What is it Bella? What's wrong?" he asked. He was seriously worried. This was what he had wanted to avoid. He didn't want her to have anything to do with any of these stuffs.

"I just talked to my brother. He said he has given the command and no one would be disobeying his orders. He wanted you dead and no way else. He said I am the only reason why the house is not yet in flame. They are here to kill you Tyrone." She was almost in tears.

"Well then I guess it is a good thing that my brother listened to me. He has agreed to let me look for a better way to solve this conflict." He looked at her and he knew what was on her mind.

"You know, when I was coming back this morning, I left my house as though I was never going to be back. I know this may break your heart but I think it would be an honor for me to die because I love you. I will die knowing that someone really loved and cared for me despite knowing who I really was." He looked at her and the tears would not stop dropping from her face.

He moved to her front, tipped her head and kissed her deep silencing every cry that escaped from her mouth. Not realizing they were still naked, Isabella's hand went down to his groin and to feel him hard was wonderful. He almost flinched when he felt her hands touch his dick. It was getting hot in between her legs and just like he knew, his fingers found its way down there again. He played with her vagina and breast, gently arousing her sexually. He knew that they would not stay out much longer. If he was to die then he would love to die on top of her. Matching each other's body, he gently fucked her and she gladly let him. She opened all of herself and accepted him.

Just at that moment, the door was broken and they rushed in.